AF292200

To

____

From

____

Date

____

A RoseKidz® Rhyming Book

Precious Blessings: What Is The Bible?
©2018 Valerie Marie Carpenter.

RoseKidz® is an imprint of
Rose Publishing, LLC
140 Summit Street
P.O. Box 3473
Peabody, Massachusetts 01961-3473
www.hendricksonrose.com

Book cover by Chad Thompson.
Illustrations by Chad Thompson
Book layout design by Keith DeDios

ISBN: 9781628625417
RoseKidz® reorder #L50014
JUVENILE NONFICTION/Religion/Devotional & Prayer
Printed in South Korea

01   4.2018.APC

What Is The Bible?

Valerie Marie Carpenter

God's Message

This is the Holy Bible.
It is my favorite book.

It's full of God's great message!
Would you like to take a look?

In the beginning, the Word was already there.
The Word was with God, and the Word was God.
—John 1:1

God's Words Written by Men

It was written long ago
By the men who heard God say,

"Please write down these words of mine."
Now, we have his words today.

The LORD said to Moses, "Write down the
words I have spoken."
—Exodus 34:27

A Love Letter from God

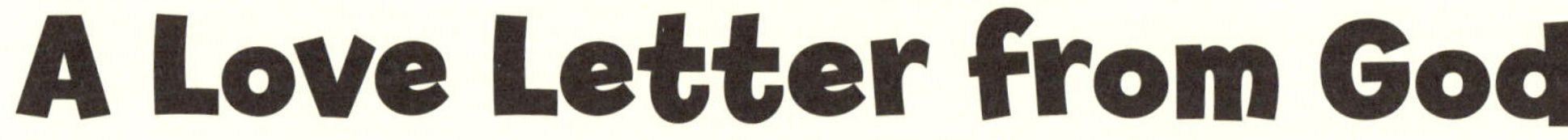

It's one great big love letter
From God, our Father, Himself.

He wants to speak to each child,
So don't leave it on your shelf!

I have hidden your word in my heart so that
I won't sin against you.
–Psalm 119:11

Instructions to Love Others

Inside you'll find many words,
But the most important part

Is to love all your neighbors
And the Lord with all your heart.

Love the Lord your God with all your heart and with all your soul.
Love him with all your mind. Love your neighbor as yourself.
—Matthew 22:37,39

Good News about Jesus

You'll learn how much God loves you,
Sending us his only Son,

Jesus Christ, to save the world.
His love is for everyone!

Holy
Bible

Light in the Darkness

Read the words of the Bible.
It's like turning on the light!

It helps you see God's way
To know what to do that's right.

Your word is like a lamp that shows me the way.
—Psalm 119:105

How to Live God's Way

Do not just hear God's good words
And forget them day by day,

But think about them deeply
So that you can live God's way.

Blessed are those who hear God's word and obey it.
—Luke 11:28

Answers from God

If you have many questions,
If you're not sure what to do,

Just open up the Bible.
God has an answer there for you!

By using Scripture, the servant of God can be completely prepared to do every good thing.
—2 Timothy 3:17

Holy Bible

Help for Life

Just like food that keeps us well
And helps us to do our best

With God's words, we grow stronger
When life puts us to the test.

*Man must not live only on bread. He must also live on
every word that comes from the mouth of God.*
—Matthew 4:4

Hope from God

If you feel like giving up
Or your heart is very sad

God's good words will give you hope. 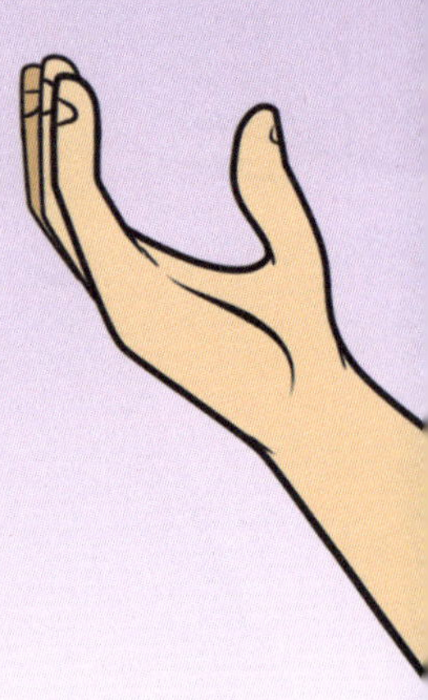
Yes, oh yes! They'll make you glad!

Be strong, all you who put your hope in the Lord.
—Psalm 31:24

Protection from Harm

If the darkness surrounds you,
God's true words are like a sword

That protect you from all harm.
You'll say, "Jesus is my Lord!"

*Put on the helmet of salvation. And take the sword
of the Holy Spirit. The sword is God's word.*
–Ephesians 6:17

Seeds for Growth

God will help you understand,
Just as you begin to read.

Each truth you learn helps you grow
Like a plant grows from a seed.

Holy
Bible

Holy
Bible

A Way to Share God with the World

When God's words live inside you
Like a light, you will glow

You'll share God's love with others
So, God the whole world will know.

*Go into all the world.
Preach the good news to everyone.*
—Mark 16:15

Treasure for Life

The Bible is God's great words!
His message is a gift for you.

Treasure each word in your heart,
Know God's love for you is true!

Let the message about Christ live
among you like a rich treasure.
—Colossians 3:16